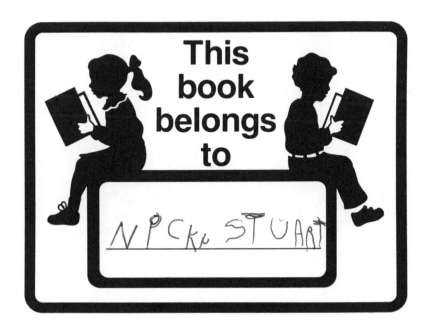

This book
belongs
to

NPCKL STUART

Henry and Mudge
IN
Puddle Trouble

The Second Book of Their Adventures

Story by Cynthia Rylant
Pictures by Suçie Stevenson

BRADBURY PRESS • NEW YORK

For the Halems:
Sandy, Henry, and Jess—CR

For Frank Modell—SS

THE HENRY AND MUDGE BOOKS

Text copyright © 1987 by Cynthia Rylant
Illustrations copyright © 1987 by Suçie Stevenson
All rights reserved. No part of this book may be reproduced or
transmitted in any form or by any means, electronic or
mechanical, including photocopying, recording or by any
information storage and retrieval system, without permission in
writing from the Publisher.

Bradbury Press
An Affiliate of Macmillan, Inc.
866 Third Avenue, New York, N.Y. 10022
Collier Macmillan Canada, Inc.

Manufactured in the United States of America
        B C D   0 1 2 3
The text of this book is set in 18 pt. Goudy Old Style.
The illustrations are watercolor and reproduced in full color.

Library of Congress Cataloging-in-Publication Data
Rylant, Cynthia.
Henry and Mudge in puddle trouble.
Summary: For Henry and his big dog Mudge, spring means
admiring the first crocus, playing in puddles in the rain, and
watching the five new kittens next door.
[1. Dogs—Fiction. 2. Spring—Fiction]. I. Stevenson,
Suçie ill. II. Title.
PZ7.R982Hk 1987 [E] 86–13616
ISBN 0-02-778002-3

Contents

The Snow Glory

When the snow melted
and Spring came,
Henry and his dog Mudge
stayed outside
all the time.

Henry had missed
riding his bike.
Mudge had missed
chewing on sticks.
They were glad
it was warmer.

One day when Henry and Mudge
were in their yard,
Henry saw something blue
on the ground.
He got closer to it.
"Mudge!" he called.
"It's a flower!"
Mudge slowly walked over
and sniffed the blue flower.

Then he sneezed
all over Henry.
"Aw, Mudge," Henry said.

Later, Henry's mother
told him that the flower
was called a snow glory.
"Can I pick it?"
Henry asked.
"Oh, no," said his mother.
"Let it grow."
So Henry didn't pick it.

Every day he saw the snow glory

in the yard,

blue

and looking so pretty.

He knew he shouldn't pick it.

He was trying not to pick it.

But he thought how nice

it would look in a jar.

He thought how nice

to bring it inside.

He thought how nice

it would be

to own that snow glory.

Every day he stood with Mudge

and looked at the flower.

Mudge would stick his nose
into the grass
all around the snow glory.
But he never looked at it
the way Henry did.
"Don't you think the snow glory
has been growing long enough?"
Henry would ask his mother.
"Let it grow, Henry,"
she would say.

Oh, Henry wanted that snow glory.

And one day

he just knew

he had to have it.

So he took Mudge

by the collar

and he stood

beside the snow glory.

"I'm going to pick it,"
Henry whispered to Mudge.
"I've let it grow a long time."
Henry bent his head and
he said in Mudge's ear,
"Now I *need* it."
And Mudge wagged his tail,
licked Henry's face,
then put his big mouth
right over that snow glory . . .

and he ate it.

"*No, Mudge!*" Henry said.

But too late.

There was a blue flower

in Mudge's belly.

"I said *need* it, not *eat* it!"
shouted Henry.
He was so mad because
Mudge took his flower.
It was Henry's flower
and Mudge took it.

And Henry almost said,
"Bad dog," but he stopped.

He looked at Mudge,
who looked back at him
with soft brown eyes
and a flower in his belly.

Henry knew it wasn't his snow glory.

He knew it wasn't anybody's snow glory.

Just a thing to let grow.

And if someone ate it,

it was just a thing to let go.

Henry stopped feeling mad.

He put his arms around
Mudge's big head.

"Next time, Mudge,"
he said,
"try to *listen* better."
Mudge wagged his tail
and licked his lips.
One blue petal
fell from his mouth
into Henry's hand.
Henry smiled,
put it in his pocket,
and they went inside.

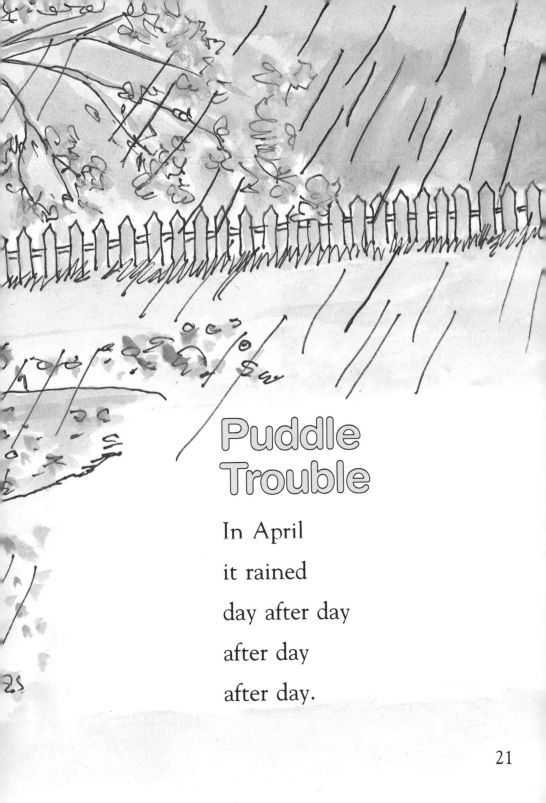

Puddle Trouble

In April
it rained
day after day
after day
after day.

Henry was getting bored.
Mudge was chewing up
everything in the house.
So Henry said,
"Let's play outside anyway."

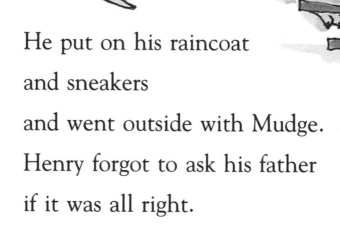

He put on his raincoat
and sneakers
and went outside with Mudge.
Henry forgot to ask his father
if it was all right.

When Mudge stepped
into the wet grass,
he lifted his paws
and shook them.
"Too bad you don't
have sneakers," Henry said.
And he walked in a circle
around Mudge.
Squish, squish, squish, squish.

Mudge listened
and looked at Henry.
Then he got closer
to Henry
and wagged his tail
and shook the water from
his big wet furry body
all over Henry.
Henry wiped the water
from his face.
"Aw, Mudge," he said.

The two of them

went walking.

And down the road

they found a big puddle.

A giant puddle.

A lake puddle.

An ocean puddle.

And Henry said, "Wow!"

He started running.

Mudge got there first.

SPLASH!

Muddy water all over Mudge.

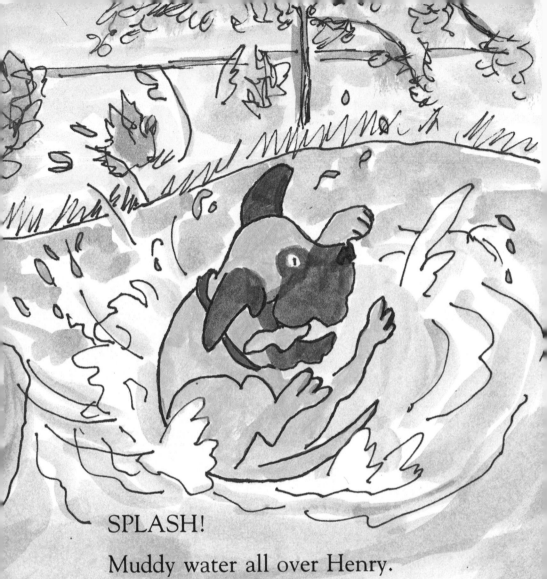

SPLASH!

Muddy water all over Henry.

It was the biggest,

deepest puddle

they had ever seen.

And they loved it.

When Henry's father
called for Henry
and didn't find him,
he went outside.
He looked down the road.
SPLASH! he heard.
He put on his raincoat
and went walking.

SPLASH! he saw.

Henry's father saw Mudge,

with a muddy face

and muddy tail

and muddy in between.

Henry's father saw Henry,
with a muddy face
and muddy sneakers
and muddy in between.
And he yelled, *"Henry!"*
No more splashes.
Just a boy and a dog,
dripping.
"Hi, Dad," Henry said,
with a little smile.
Mudge wagged his tail.
"Henry, you know
you should have asked me first,"
Henry's father said.
"I know," said Henry.

"I am surprised at you,"
Henry's father said.
"I'm sorry," said Henry.
"I don't know what to do
with you," Henry's father said.
Henry looked sad.
Then Mudge wagged his tail,
licked Henry's hand,
and shook the water
from his big wet furry body
all over Henry and Henry's father.

"*Mudge!*" Henry yelled.

Henry's father stood there

with a muddy face

and muddy shoes

and muddy in between.

He looked at Mudge,

he looked at Henry,

he looked at the big puddle.

Then he smiled.

"Wow," he said.

And he jumped in.

He splashed water on Mudge.

He splashed water on Henry.

He said, "Next time, ask me along!"

Henry said, "Sure, Dad."

And Henry splashed him back.

The Kittens

In May the cat who lived
next door to Henry and Mudge
had a litter of kittens.
There were five kittens.
One was orange.
One was gray.
One was black and white.
And two were all black.

The kittens sometimes stayed

in a box in their front yard

to get some sun

while the mother cat rested.

One day Henry and Mudge

peeked in the box.

They saw tiny little

kitten faces

and tiny little

kitten paws

and heard tiny little

kitten meows.

Mudge sniffed
and sniffed and sniffed.
He wagged his tail
and sneezed
and sniffed some more.
Then he put his
big head into the box
and with his big tongue
he licked
all five kittens.

Henry laughed.

"Do you want

some kittens of your own?"

he asked Mudge.

Mudge grunted

and wagged his tail again.

Whenever the kittens

were in their front yard,

Henry and Mudge

visited the box.

Henry loved their

little noses.

And he had even

given them names.

He called them
Venus,
Earth,
Mars,
Jupiter,
and Saturn.
Henry loved planets, too.

While Henry was at school one day,

a new dog came up Henry's street.

The five kittens

were sleeping

in the box in their yard.

Mudge was sleeping in Henry's house.

When the new dog
got closer to Henry's house,
Mudge's ears went up.

When the new dog
got even closer
to Henry's house,
Mudge's nose went in the air.
And just when the new dog
was in front of
Henry's house,
Mudge barked.

He barked and barked
and barked
until Henry's mother
opened the door.

And just as
Mudge ran out the door,
the new dog
was in the neighbor's yard,
looking in the kittens' box.
And just as the new dog
was putting his big teeth into the box,
Mudge ran up behind him.

SNAP! went Mudge's teeth
when the new dog saw him.
SNAP! went Mudge's teeth again
when the new dog looked back
at the box of kittens.

Mudge growled.

He looked into the eyes of the new dog.

He stood ready to jump.

And the new dog backed away
from the box.

He didn't want the kittens anymore.

He just wanted to leave.

And he did.

Mudge looked in the kitten box.
He saw five tiny faces
and five skinny tails
and twenty little paws.
He reached in and licked
all five kittens.

Then he lay down
beside the box
and waited for Henry.
Venus,
Earth,
Mars,
Jupiter,
and Saturn
went back to sleep.